Y0-CUO-133

This story is dedicated to all librarians and bookstore owners out there. Your wisdom brings happiness to countless people. THANK YOU!

José Carlos Andrés

The Mouse Who Ate Books
Somos8 Series

© Text: José Carlos Andrés, 2015/2023
© Illustrations: Katharina Sieg, 2015/2023
© Edition: NubeOcho, 2023
www.nubeocho.com · hello@nubeocho.com

Original Title: *El ratón que comía cuentos*
Translation: Cecilia Ross
English Editing: Caroline Dookie, Rebecca Packard

First Edition: October, 2023
ISBN: 978-84-19607-30-0
Legal Deposit: M-4903-2023

Printed in Portugal.

All rights reserved.

The Mouse
Who Ate Books

José Carlos Andrés   Katharina Sieg

nubeOCHO

Klaus was a teeny-tiny, big-eared, stubby-legged, short-whiskered mouse.

He ate lots of cheese sandwiches on bread and bread sandwiches on cheese. But no matter how much he ate, his stomach always felt empty.

Was this what people called hunger?

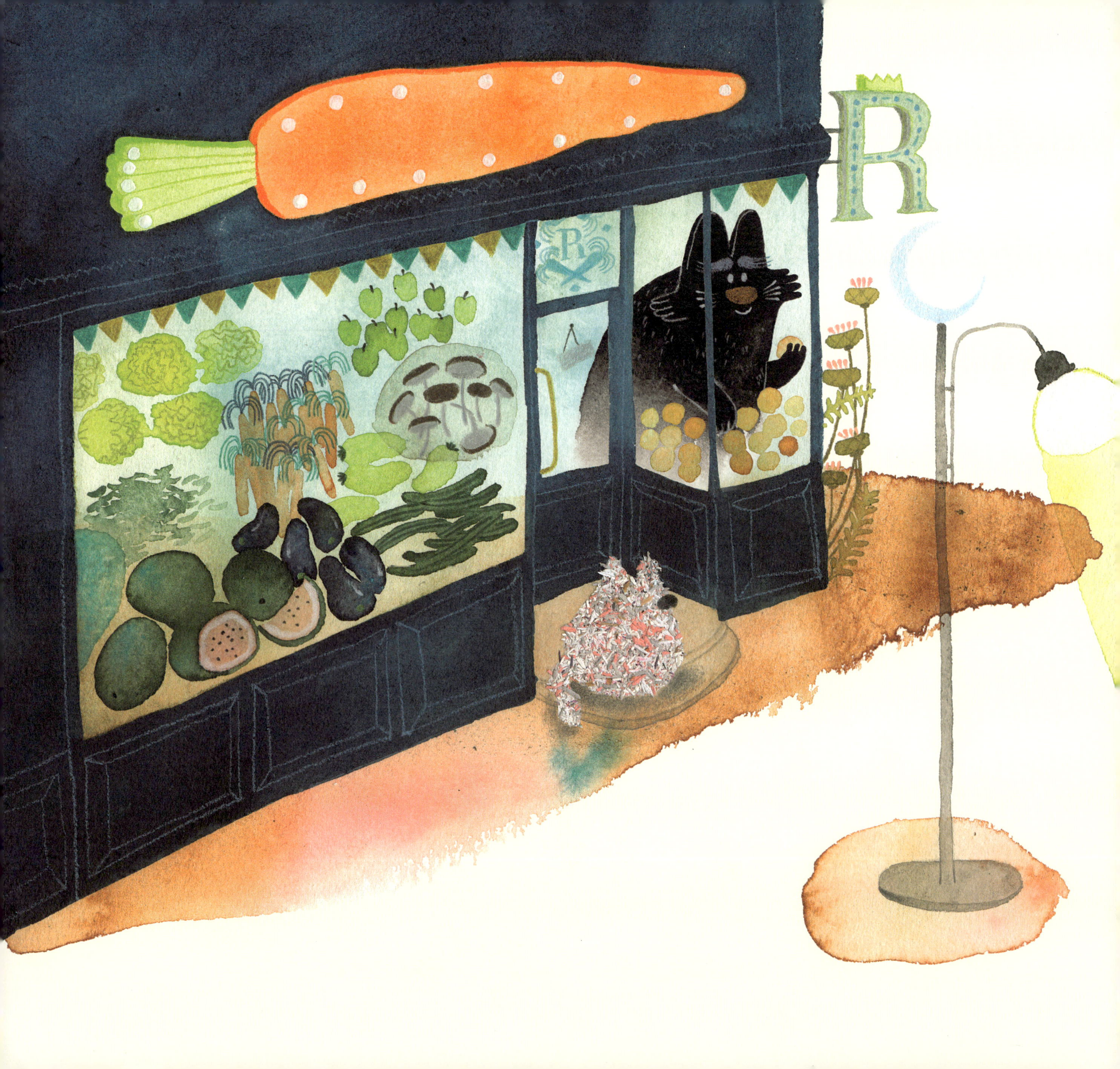
R

One day, he set off in search of more food to eat. He stopped at a fruit store and tried some apples and grapes. He liked them.

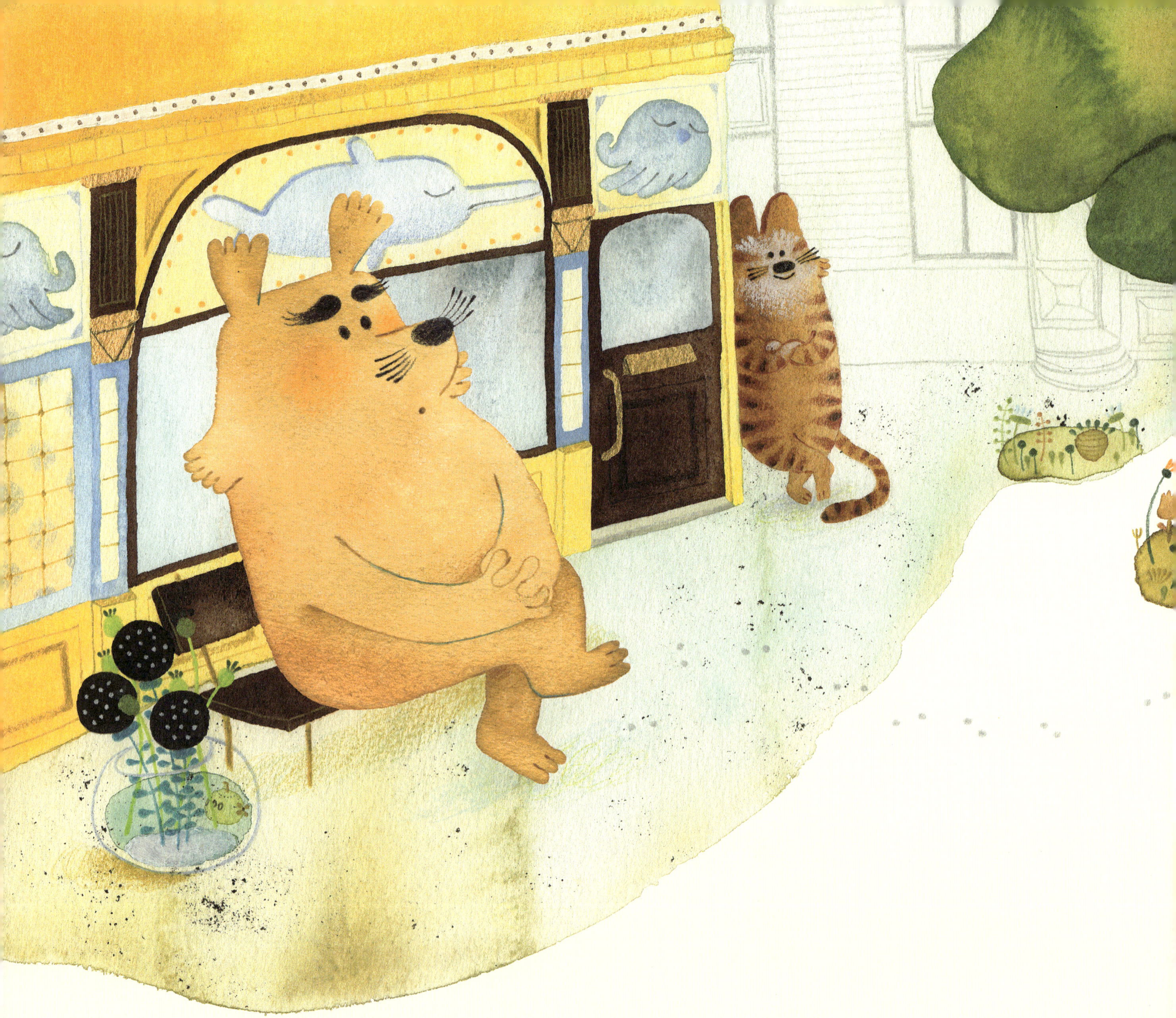

Next he came to the fishmonger's, which was the cats' favorite, and there he sampled hake, trout, and salmon (which was the bears' favorite). Everything was delicious, but he still had a hollow feeling deep inside his belly. Was this hunger?

Then Klaus stumbled across a bookstore.

"I wonder what they have to eat here?" he thought to himself.

He scurried inside,
and he heard someone saying,

"If I don't start selling some books soon,
I may as well let the mice eat them all."

This convinced Klaus he should try some. He began by taking a few little nibbles out of some picture books. They tasted like blue beards, green pixies, and red riding hoods… They were so yummy!

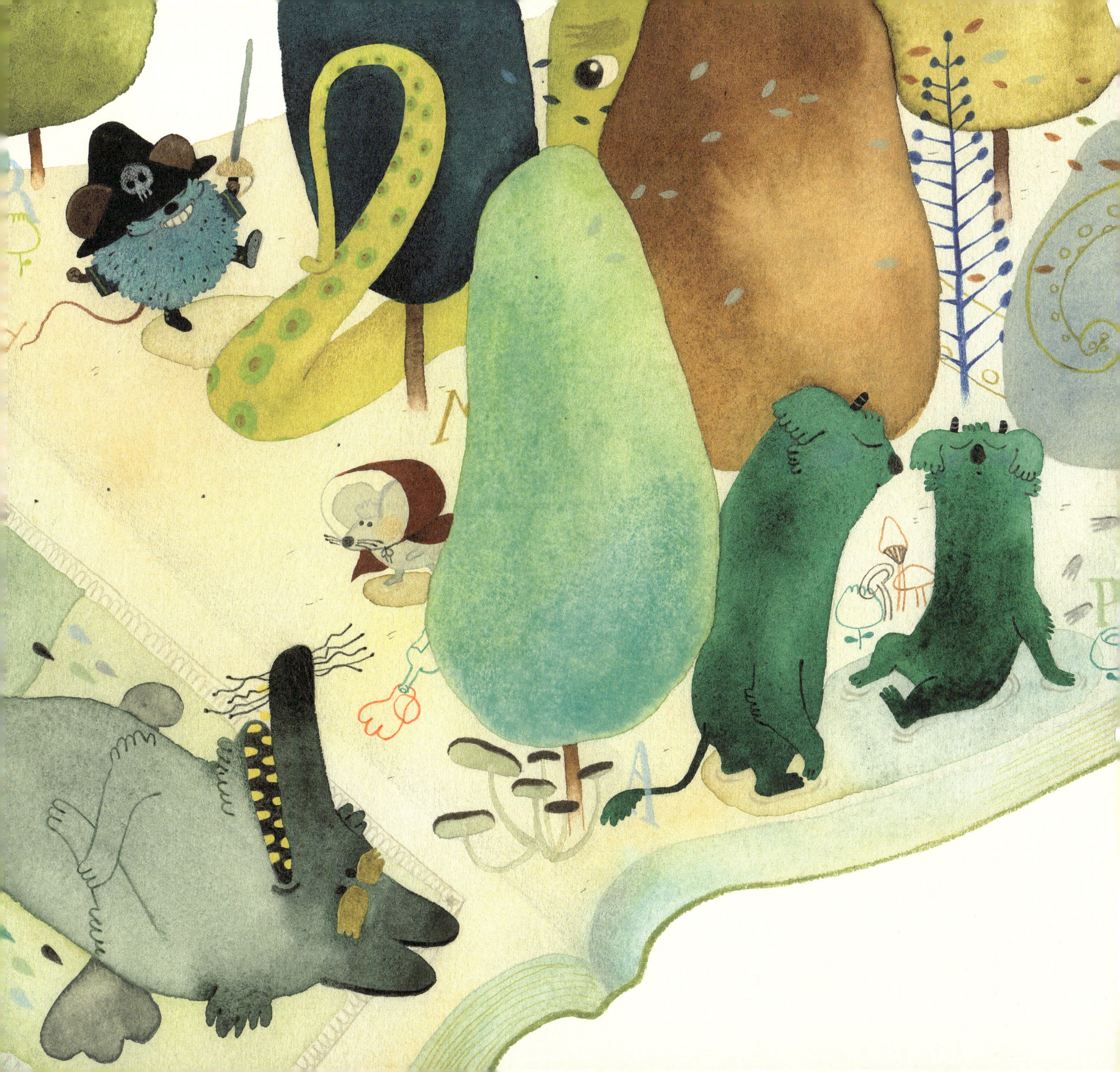

Next he tried some with lots of words. These ones tasted like adventures, pirate ships, and hidden treasures. They were delicious!

For the first time in his life,
he felt truly full,
and he fell happily asleep.

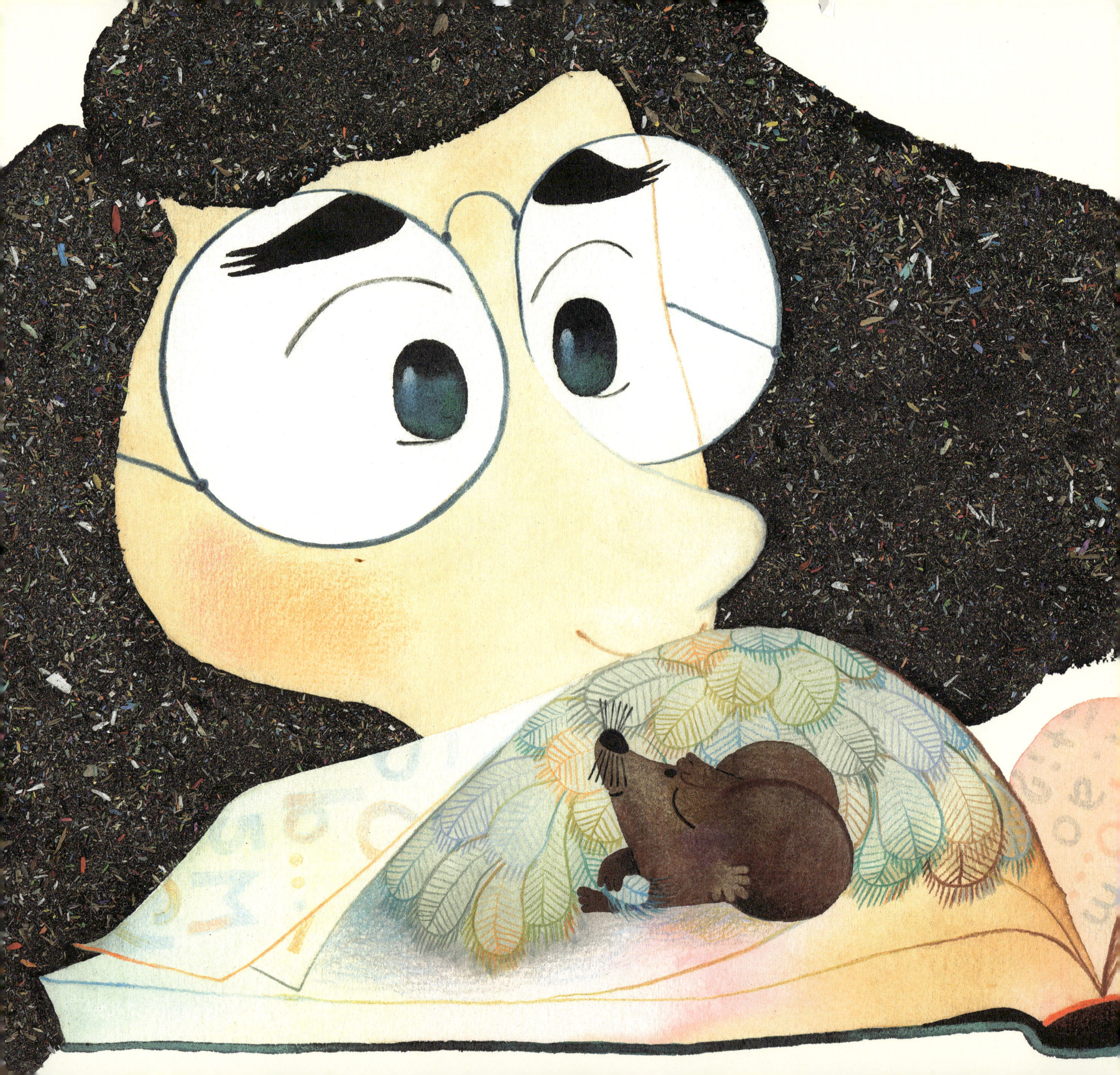

When he woke up, he saw two enormous bespectacled eyes staring back at him.

"You don't have to eat the books. I can read them to you until you know how," the bookstore owner told him.

Klaus was a little frightened at first, but then he saw that in those eyes there were thousands more adventures and new worlds to discover.

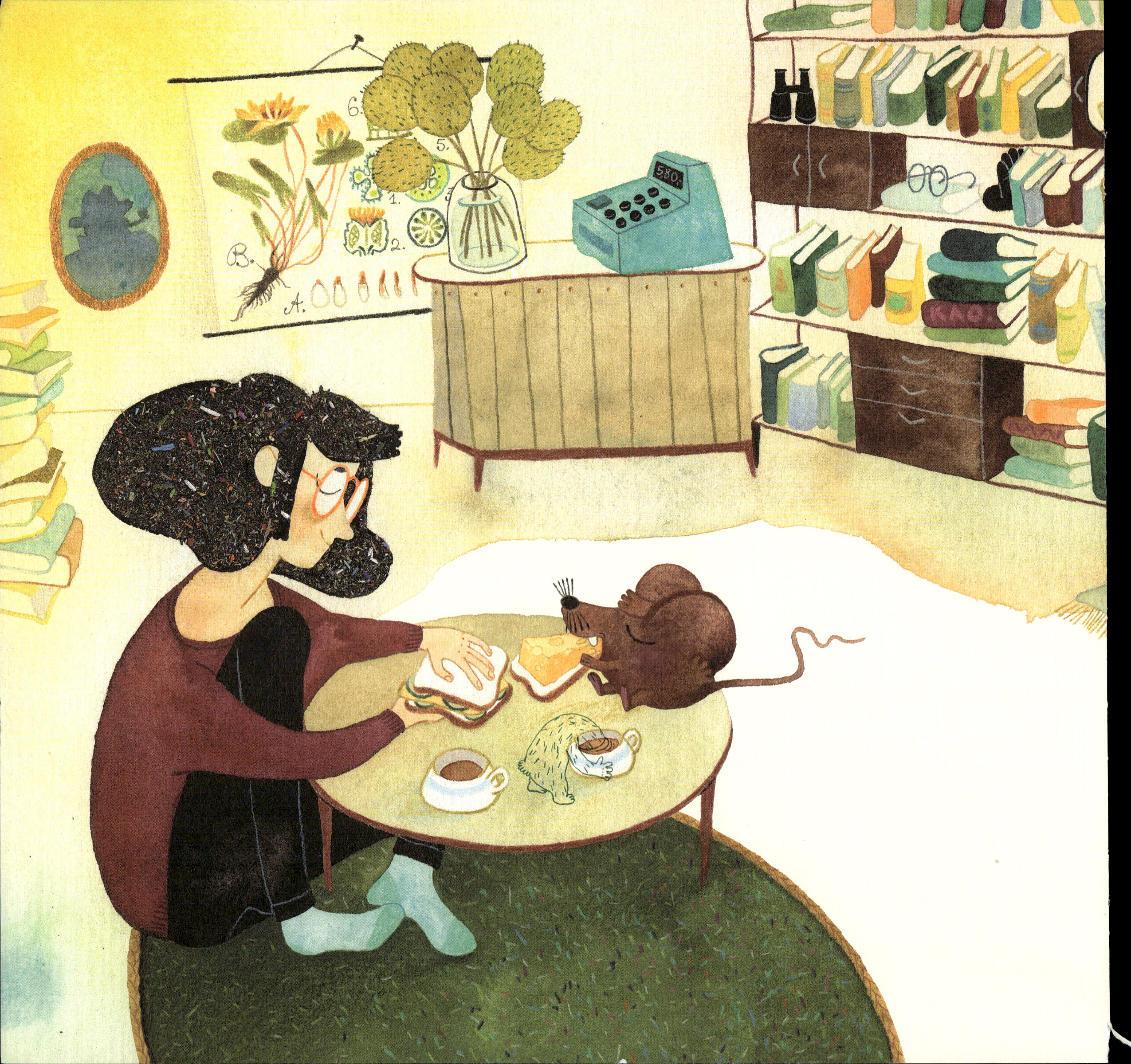
6.
5.
1.
2.
B.
A.
580.
KAO.

They shared a piece of bread with cheese (and then a piece of cheese with bread) and then they came to an agreement: Klaus would lend a hand at the bookstore, and in exchange, she would read him stories, tales, and adventures.

That night, the bookstore owner read him a story
about a piper who was followed everywhere
he went by crowds of rats and children.
The little mouse liked this story a lot,
and it gave him a great idea.

Klaus scampered off to find his friend
Johann Strauss the Mouse, who was
a great musician, and he told him his plan.

The next morning, Johann Strauss the Mouse came striding toward the bookstore, playing a tune on a bamboo flute. Dozens of girls and boys and mice and other animals were following him.

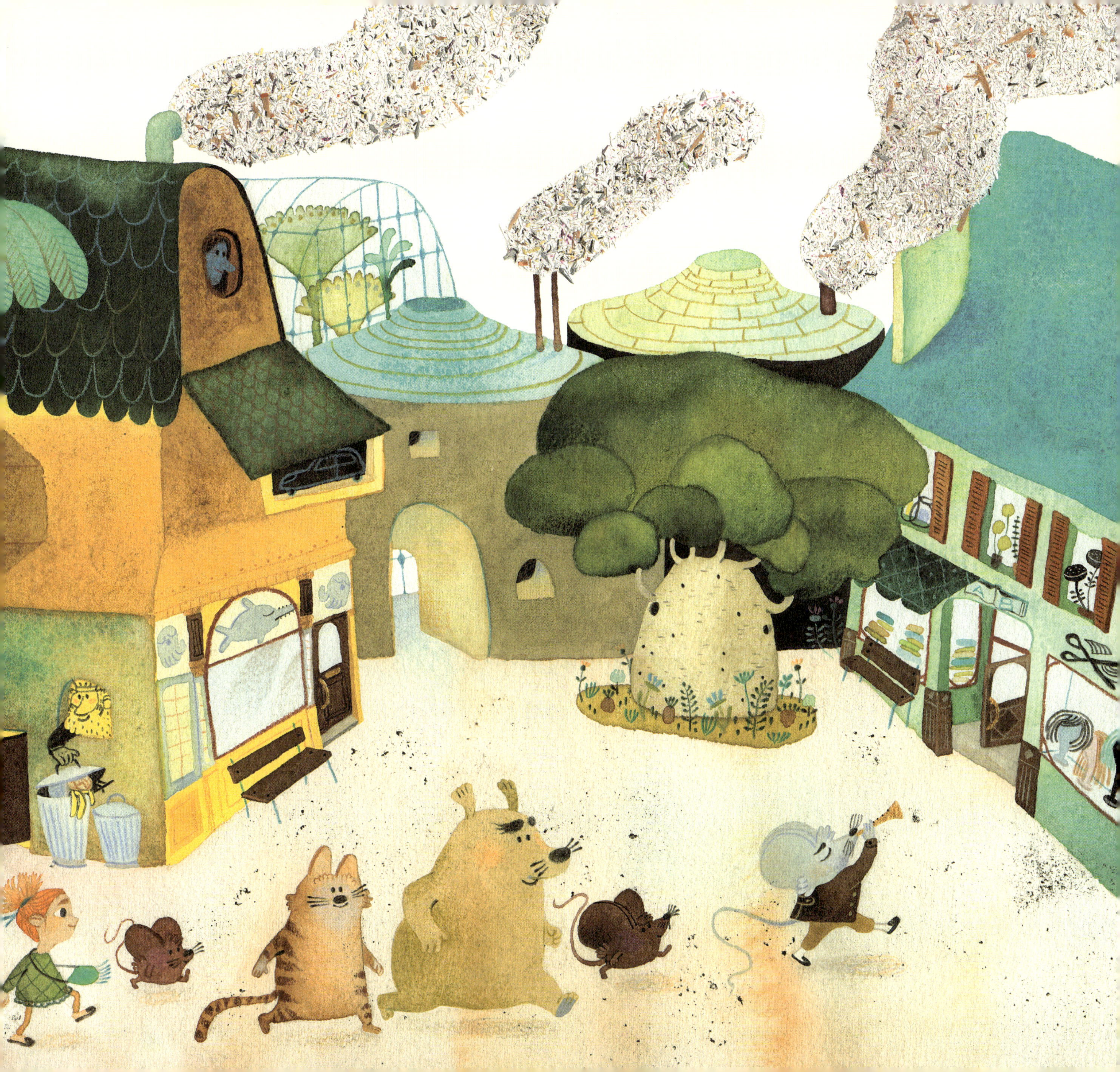

Moments later, the bookstore owner and
Klaus were busy handing out books
and recommendations left, right, and center.

And that night, the bookstore owner
read story after story to all the dozens of
girls and boys and mice and other animals.
Until that day, they had all felt the same
unfillable emptiness as Klaus had.

But now they all understood:
they were hungry for stories.

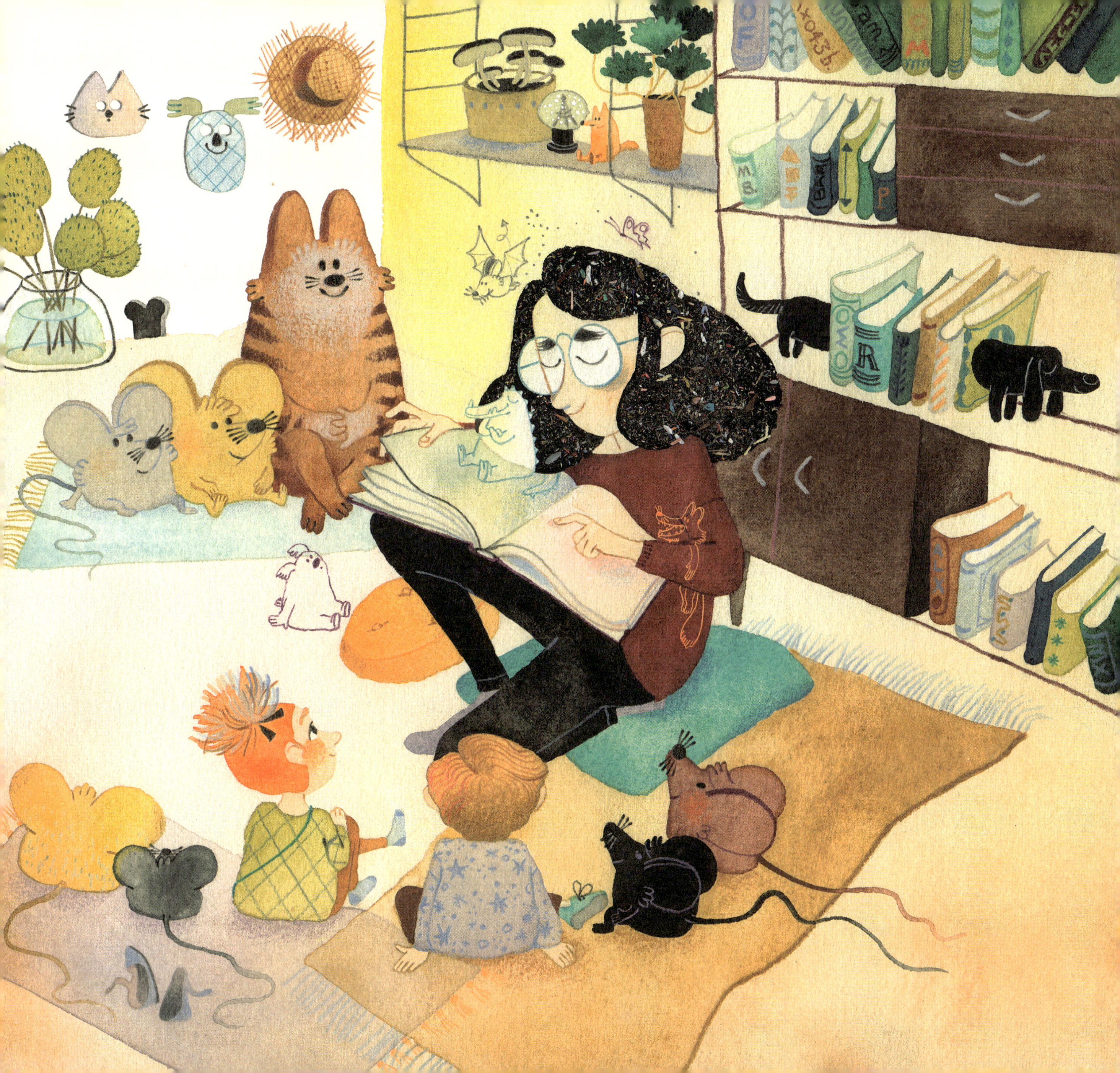

In the evening, when Klaus and the bookstore owner were alone, she asked him,

"So you lured them here, just like the Pied Piper of Hamelin?"

The mouse winked at her, cracked open a book, and began reading aloud,

"Once upon a time…"

He no longer felt any hollowness inside, because he was full to bursting with stories, tales, and adventures. And he never felt hungry again.

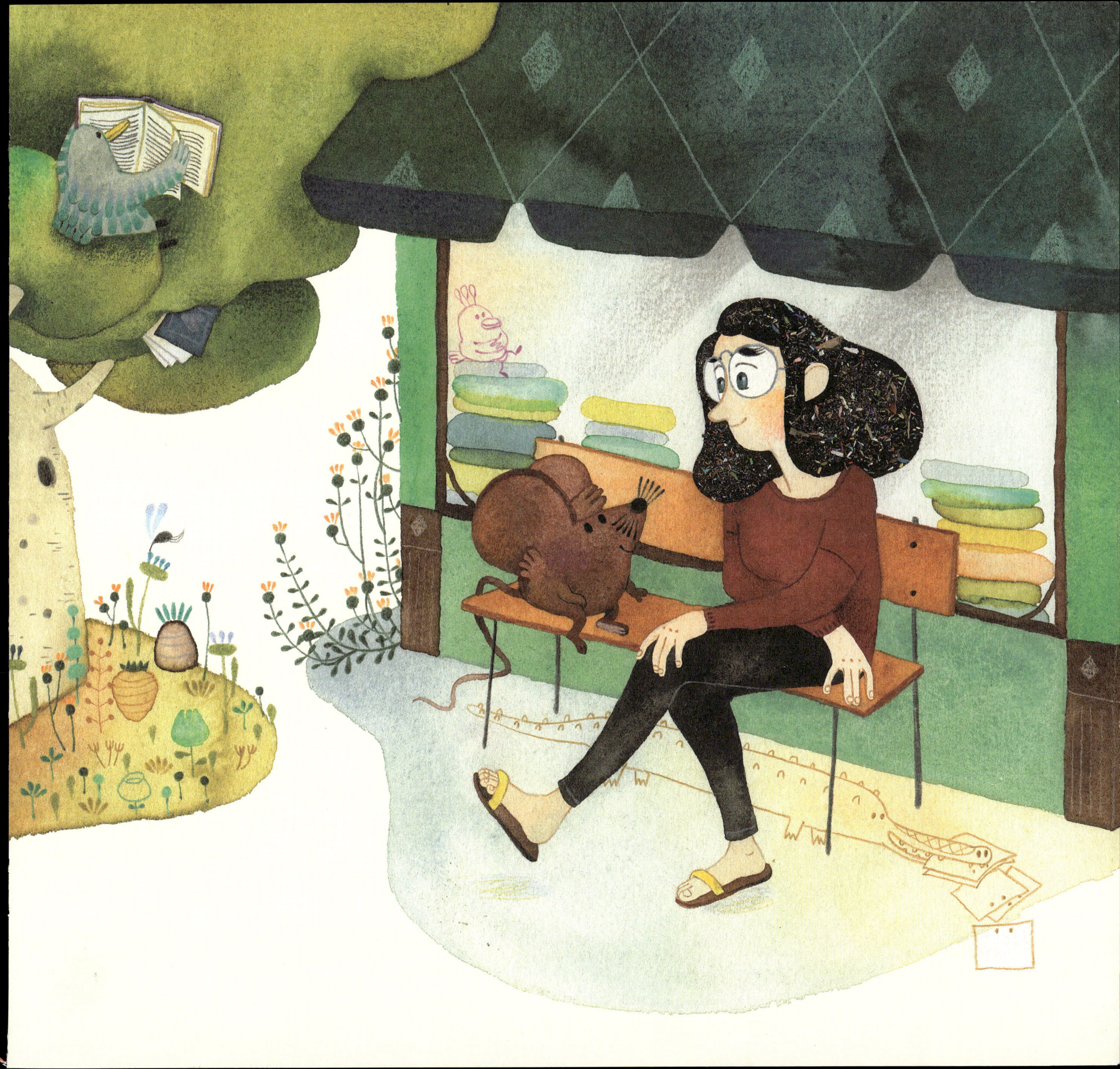